BULLETS, BLADES, AND HIGH HEELS

BULLETS, BLADES, AND HIGH HEELS

Pulp Fiction Stories

PHIL GERRAUD

BULLETS, BLADES, AND HIGH HEELS
Pulp Fiction Stories

Copyright © 2019 Phil Gerraud

This book is a work of fiction. Names, characters, places, and events are either products of the author's imagination or are used fictitiously. Any resemblance to actual events or places or persons, living or dead, is purely coincidental.

ISBN 979-12-200-4792-0

Second printing 2021

Cover design: Piers Tilbury

Dedicated to someone …

For she was beautiful: her beauty made
The bright world dim, and everything beside
Seemed like the fleeting image of a shade …

—Percy Bysshe Shelley, *The Witch of Atlas*

CONTENTS

After a Heavy Snowfall

She takes a quick shower, brushes her long black hair, puts on her make-up—just a little, though—and she walks to the window. For a moment she once again sees droves of children scampering around the streets on their holidays when the schools were shut, or playing football from pavement to pavement, challenging the few cars parked there. She stirs and the scene soon changes; she realises everything has become white outside. It is late autumn, but it has snowed all night. She is not familiar at all with this natural magic. She had always lived elsewhere, where snowfall had been only an improbable dream. Strangely, the fact she is no longer living where she used to comes to her now as a renewed revelation, although she had moved here several months ago. She now resides in this small town in the south of England, and she is where her heart has led her. She sighs and dashes downstairs, the wooden steps creaking as she runs. She puts on her boots, coat, woollen cap, scarf, and gloves, and out she rushes. She had received a text message earlier that morning.

After a heavy snowfall, the world is different. Ghostly. Eerie. There are only a few people around. She strides across a vast square, heading for Costa Coffee. She enters the café, and it is warm inside. Someone is expecting her, sitting at a corner table. He wanted to see her. He said he would have to talk to her. She walks over to him. He looks up at her and winks. She takes off her gloves, scarf, and cap, places them on the table, and sits down without saying a word of greeting. A mug of smoking black tea is ready there for her.

"I ordered your favourite tea," he says. "I knew you'd be punctual."

"I always am," she says. Her eyes are fiery because of the frosty early morning air.

"I'm surprised you agreed to see me."

"I had to."

"I know I disappointed you, and I'm sorry," he says. "You moved here because of me. But things have never been all right between us, after all. These past few days away from you, after our umpteenth row, have made me understand one thing: we are too different. That's a fact."

"What do you mean to do?" she asks, clasping the mug of hot tea, as if to warm her hands.

"I'm going to leave you for ever."

"I appreciate your honesty," she tells him, lowering her gaze and watching the steam rising from her tea. "Actually, I'd already decided you had to go."

A scornful look appears on his face. "You don't accept defeat, do you?"

"I never lose," she says, raising her eyes and peering at him.

"A blonde has defeated you this time. I love her."

A painful frown wrinkles her forehead. "She's a fake blonde, and you know it."

He smiles and shrugs. He makes as if to stand up and leave.

"Hold on," she says, before he gets up. "I'm only

angry with myself. You don't even deserve my anger. I still don't understand why I thought I could love a guy like you—someone who falls for a slut who tampers with nature."

His mouth opens, but she does not let him retort. Her right hand crawls down and pulls a microscopic revolver out of her coat pocket. Almost a toy. His eyes snap open in disbelief. The shot is no louder than a child's cough. One of his eyes blows apart, while the other's stare remains glued on her. His brain has not yet realised it is dead, and so for a moment he keeps gawking at her. A second later, he thumps down head first on the table. She slides the revolver back in her pocket and takes up her mug before the stream of blood oozing from his now-vacant eye socket touches it. Her tea is still hot. She does not hear the people screaming around her. It is a perfect early morning after a heavy snowfall. Quiet and cosy.

She closes her eyes and starts sipping at her favourite tea.

A Blue Motorbike

It's a cloudy, but clammy late summer evening. Another boring evening following an eventless day. No client. I need one damn badly. That plaque outside my office seems useless—*P. G. Private Investigations*. I haven't had such a slump in my activity in years. I have to work on something as soon as possible, or my job will be on the line. Whisky isn't going to be of any help, but it's better than nothing. I always have a bottle on my bookcase, next to my criminology tomes. The moment I'm about to uncork it, my office door bursts open, and she storms in. How long has it been since I saw such a stunner? Slinky blood-red mini-dress, stilettos, lipstick, all perfectly matched; her extravagant chandelier earrings scattering streamers of glitter all around. My jaw drops.

Is this a dick's office or a nightclub? I think. I place the whisky bottle back on the shelf and seat myself behind my desk, trying to appear as professional as possible.

She struts up to me. Her swaying bum causes a soft breeze to blow. Her body talks before she utters a word. *I'm already listening, baby!* I think.

"Let me guess," she says, or perhaps I just suppose she's saying something rather than actually hearing her words. "You're thinking I need help, aren't you?"

I pull myself together. I shake my head. I don't know whether I'm listening to the sound of her voice or the vibrations of her legs and hips.

"I think you need trouble," I say.

She laughs. "Are you able to serve it?"

"I'll make your day. You want me to take snaps of your husband in bed with his lover, don't you? I'm very good at that. Spying on people in their love nests, I mean."

"My case is not so ordinary."

"Your boss's arse, then. You wanna nail it 'cos you wanna blackmail him, don't you?"

She shakes her head, blows me a kiss, and sits on the corner of my desk. "Listen, I've got a blue motorbike in my garage. It broke down a few months back."

"So, you don't need a dick, but a garage stud."

"It's complicated," she says, crossing her legs. *Christ! How can she do that without losing her balance?*

"I don't get you." I scratch the back of my head and squint at the bottle of whisky on the shelf. I'm parched and am now in need of a shot.

"Actually, that motorbike isn't mine," she says, "but I'm itching to sell it all the same. The fact is, *he* doesn't want me to."

"*Who* doesn't want you to sell it?"

"That's none of your business, sweetie."

"With those legs of yours, it'd be a piece of cake for you to talk *him* round to your plans."

She leans in towards me, and her blood-red mini-dress is so generous that it doesn't bother to hide her heavenly cleavage.

"Old boy," she says, "you don't seem to be too perceptive."

"No?" I growl. "Why don't you hire a skilful bore to fix your bloody motorbike in the first place?"

"That would only solve *part* of my problems."

I'm dying to be in control, but I don't have a clue. I blush and scratch the back of my head again.

"I may have missed something," I tell her.

"Sure. That's why you're starving in this lousy shack."

My face grows purple. I fidget on the chair and want her to take back those offensive words, but she doesn't let me object.

She leans in much closer and in a soft voice she mutters, "I'd like you to put a bullet in *his* head."

S&S

Night in a desert is chilly, even in summer. Like something from a horror cartoon, the moon is an enormous ivory skull hanging over a pitch-black canvas. The neon sign is blinking without pause: 'Dreamland—Open 24/7.' I've always wondered why someone decides to open up a dive hundreds of miles away from humankind. But the most absurd thing is, I carry on idling my nights away in this place in the middle of nowhere. Always the same table by the window. Always the same bottle of rum. It's damn late now, and the lamps are giving out no palpable light. A vintage jukebox in a corner has been spewing out lugubrious music for hours. This dump never shuts, and the bartender never knocks off working. I am trying to write, sitting by the window. I always try to write something in front of a bottle of rum and a brimful glass. It's a universal law. Alcohol is my muse.

When I hear the unearthly wail of brakes and tyres, I look out of the window. A silver Ferrari has pulled up in the yard. Out of a typhoon of dust, a dark-haired lady emerges. She's wearing a slate-grey Saint Laurent suit and pumps. She swaggers into the dive and orders a mango squash with tequila and a pinch of cinnamon. The skinny bartender complies straight away, and she snatches her cocktail and immediately starts sipping. As soon as she's done this, she stops, turns her head, and glances at me. Our eyes meet. I spot a gold brooch on her lapel—it reads S&S—and I recognise the notorious logo, feared by most writers on earth.

"Shit!" I grumble. "That bloody posh literary critic."

She notices I'm writing, slams down her glass on the counter, and parades over, her heels clacking on the floor.

"I'm S," she says, standing right in front of me. "I sense creative vibrations in the air."

"What does the other 's' stand for?" I dare ask.

"You're far too curious," she says. "What are you writing?"

"A poem," I answer.

Her dark-grey eyes, and her slate-grey suit and pumps are too much for this place; too much for the people lying back here and gawping at her.

"Hmm … I can either help you or destroy you," she says. "Are you a good poet?"

"No," I say, fighting not to stare at her. "Poetry is too painful sometimes."

"Poetry doesn't even sell," she says. "But would you dedicate a poem to me?"

Yeah, she is too much for everything.

"Right now I'm trying to write this ode. It's dedicated to a mysterious nymph I bumped into at an underground station."

"My poets only write poems for me. For no other sluts!"

"I could write a whole *Divine Comedy* for you. A whole *Divine Comedy*, do you get that? But the bloody fact is, if I did, would you even have time to read it?"

She shrugs indifferently.

"Now," she says, changing the subject, "I'm just fed up with driving my Ferrari myself. I only need someone who can drive me around. Yes, can drive me around the world and tell me stories nobody has ever told me before."

"That person isn't me," I blurt out, and I knock back my rum.

She squints at me and shakes her head mockingly. She steps closer, bends forwards, and grabs my bottle of rum with a satanic sneer of contempt deforming her ruthless face.

"Sophisticated blend, eh?" she says, lifting the bottle and admiring its label, or just pretending to do so. "It's a pity I've got to waste it."

I have no strength left to stand up and prevent her from doing what she means to. Spellbound, I watch her tilt the bottle over and pour all that precious liquor onto the floor. When something spurs me on and I spring to my feet, it's too late. My bottle of rum is now empty in her grasp.

"How could you dare?" I roar.

She snickers, still holding the bottle by its neck, and whacks me on the head with its base. I fall to the floor, waves of horrific pain criss-crossing my entire body. Probably my head has smashed into pieces like a flowerpot hit by a mattock. I moan, but nobody helps me. I cannot see anything. I just feel her hand grabbing my hair and pulling my head up like a safari trophy. Then I think I hear her fruity voice whisper something in my ear: "Now, stand up and do what you've got to do. My Ferrari is waiting for you outside. I've got a long way to go and no time to lose."

Cyril's Sister

The stench of cheap cigarettes is unbearable in this pub in the dock area, but I don't give a toss. Tonight I've bet I'll knock back ten pints of stout in half an hour and I mean to win. Cyril is a sly bugger, and he has managed to trick me into this insane endeavour. I've only known Cyril for a couple of hours, but I've already told him about my whole life and he has already told me about his. Cyril is one of those desperate souls I run across in pubs and who stick to me like bluebottles to rotten meat. However, you wouldn't say such an octopus of a man—slimy and obese— could have such a gorgeous sister. Yeah, Cyril is an abnormal mountain of lipids and sweat, but he has a sister and she is a jewel. Her name is Siobhan. Thin, petite, with a fleece of long red hair, and emerald eyes. A top-class young chick. Well, I don't know her personally, but during the first hour of our casual friendship, Cyril told me everything about her, and now it's as if I have already met her. He even showed me lots of photos and videos of her in shorts or bikini, and one where she was dancing on the beach at sunset.

"Let's have a bet," Cyril had suggested to me suddenly. "If you down ten pints in half an hour, they'll all be on me. Plus, I'll phone Siobhan and persuade her to date you."

"Who are you, mate? A pimp?" I burst out.

"Hell, no!" Cyril had snapped. "Just bet. You've got nothing to lose."

"And if I fail?"

"Nothing."

"*Nothing*? What the hell is this? You kidding, eh?"

"No. We're friends, aren't we?"

"Yeah, right. What proof is there that bloody sister of yours will date me?"

"She will. She'll fancy you," Cyril said, and his face turned into a satyr's.

"She's a whore, isn't she?" I said.

"Hell, no!" he exclaimed again.

I didn't believe him, but I wasn't able to stand up and walk away. I accepted this hellish bet of his, which now I've just about managed to pull off. Yeah, I've been drinking stout for the last half-hour, and this is my last pint. When I finally see the bottom of this bloody glass, I chuck it down on the table and shout, "Phone that bloody sister of yours, wanker!"

Cyril scratches his head, his face a mask of sweat.

"On second thoughts," he mumbles, "you might not like her. I'm sorry. We shouldn't have bet."

"What the hell are you saying now? She's got beautiful eyes, hair, boobs, bum, and legs. I love her!"

"I promised her I wouldn't do these things again," he says.

I grab him by his shirt collar, and as I shake him a shower of sweat sprinkles on me, but I don't give a damn. "You're chickening out, eh?" I yell. "Get your bloody phone and ring her!"

Cyril has just pulled out his mobile when a red-haired bitch storms into the pub and swaggers up to our table, which is adorned with ten empty pint glasses and spilt stout.

"Crap!" Cyril exclaims. "Siobhan."

She's as gorgeous as in her photos. She's wearing a red T-shirt with the image of Yogi Bear deformed by her massive boobs, a red miniskirt, and red platform heels. Yeah, Siobhan is thin and not very tall, but her boobs are massive.

"What on earth are you doing here, Cyril?" she spits, standing by our table, arms akimbo. She doesn't even seem to notice I'm there. "We're behind with our schedule and you're wasting your time filling your stomach with this shit."

"We just made a bet," Cyril stutters. "I lost. But I promise I won't do it again."

Siobhan darts a glance at the ten empty pint glasses scattered on the table in front of us. "The usual bet, isn't it?"

Cyril shakes his head guiltily like a five-year-old child caught doing something mischievous. "No. I just bet you'd date this bloke this time."

"*This time?*" I ask her.

Siobhan shoots me a glance. "Yep. He's been doing this for two months, since he escaped from his mental hospital."

"What?"

"Yep," she tells me. "He'd been locked in for over twenty years, and then he escaped. Cyril's a nutcase."

"No, I'm not," Cyril protests.

"Yes, you are," she says. "Last week you wished for me to marry a Mormon widower."

"Wh-what? And did you do it?" I ask her.

"Of course I didn't," Siobhan jibes.

I'm not feeling comfortable anymore. I stand up.

"I think I've heard enough," I say. "I must be off."

"Where are you going," Cyril says. "You've won. You've got to date my sister."

Siobhan grasps my wrist. "You're going nowhere."

"What?"

"Cyril's a blabbermouth," Siobhan says. "He might have blabbed about our plans."

"What plans?"

She frowns and an evil smirk materialises on her lips. "That stout is taking its toll on you, isn't it? Are you with us or against us?"

"What the hell are you talking about?" I say, trying to get free from her grip, which is damn tight.

She pulls at my wrist and forces me to stop struggling. "Everything is wrong around us. There's no longer justice." She's staring at me now, her eyes getting darker and darker, deeper and deeper.

"There's never been any," I dare to say.

"You're a cynical bastard," she says. "*We* are the only way out." And her grip becomes an infernal vice.

"What do you mean?"

She leans in and whispers, "We're going to take over the world."

My jaw drops. "You're insane."

But I have no time to do anything more because I feel the barrel of her gun pressing into my side, forcing me to do whatever the hell she has in mind.

Herbert, a Peevish Bitch, and I

Herbert and I have been friends since elementary school. Then he left for Vietnam to work as a waiter there. You may ask why he picked out Vietnam, but I haven't got the slightest idea, and I've always asked myself the same question. However, he flew there, but he only managed to find a job as a dishwasher, nothing more. Eventually, he met a nightclub waitress, they got married, and when a few months later they divorced, he flew back home. Now he works in a Turkish restaurant, and his boss is a peevish bitch of Scottish origin, but his dream has come true at last. He has become a waiter. Incidentally, those are not my words, but his. *A peevish bitch*, this is exactly the way he described her.

"And I've fallen for her," he confessed to me last week, while we were having a pint at the corner pub. "Those muscular legs in high heels. And her voice, that voice of hers …"

"What about her voice?"

"When she bites my head off, it's a sharp blade that kisses my neck."

"And you like it?"

"I love it," he said. "But she's married. She's *damn* married."

"Great. You're in trouble for more than one reason."

"I know," he sighed.

"No, you don't."

"It's because she's a married woman, isn't it?" he said.

"It's not that," I told him.

"Is it because I may end up with a knife stuck in my stomach then?"

"Maybe you will," I said. "But I didn't mean that either."

"Is it because she's so damn irritable?"

"No. Not even because of that."

"So what then?" he burst out.

"It's because of her name," I said.

"Don't you like her name? *Alphonsine MacCate*. Isn't it captivating? Such a sweet melange of French and Scottish."

"Well, her Christian name and surname give her away."

"What do you mean?" he asked.

"Probably she's got real French blood in her veins. Probably her great-great-great etc. grandfather even came from Paris," I said.

"What the hell are you talking about?"

"You aren't familiar with Edgar Allan Poe, are you?"

"Hey, pal, we're in a pub here, drinking beer and talking about a bitch—OK, the bitch I love—but that's got nothing to do with this literary crap."

"Listen, Herbert, and be amazed at the outcome," I told him. Then I downed my pint, wiped my mouth with the back of my hand, and started, "I love Poe's 'The Gold-Bug,' and I studied linguistics and the phonetic changes in words at university, and all that can help me unravel the mystery hidden in your Alphonsine MacCate's name."

Herbert shook his head, but said, "Fire away. I'm curious."

"Everybody knows," I began, "the prefix *Mac* or *Mc* in British surnames means *son of*, which may be the prefix *De* if translated into French. *Cate* is usually pronounced *Kate* with a hard C, but suppose we pronounced it with a soft C instead. We'd have *Sate*. Suppose now that originally the dental T wasn't actually a T, but another dental consonant—let's say D. The final result wouldn't be so difficult to guess if you put everything together. *De Sade*! It's damn shocking, isn't it? And this, my dear Herbert, may account for most of your Alphonsine's eccentricities."

A Romantic Picnic

I've chosen an idyllic spot in this suburban park for my first picnic with her. It's early June, mild and clear, and only a soft sea breeze disturbs our hair. Goldfinches are warbling in the ash trees; in the distance a few children are flying butterfly-shaped kites on the lawn, a young mum is having a stroll with her baby in the pram, and an elderly couple are walking their dog.

I spread a tartan blanket on the grass, unfold a collapsible table and two stools, and lay out small chocolate cakes, a picnic teapot, two saucers, cups, and silver teaspoons.

"The tea is still hot, honey," I tell her.

"Is it strong?" she asks.

"Yes. Earl Grey. Black, strong, and bitter."

She squints at me. She is wearing green shorts and a floral blouse. If Botticelli were here, he would add her to his *Allegory of Spring* without hesitation.

"Hmm," she says. "A fairy-tale place, black tea, chocolate cakes. You seem to know me very well."

I chuckled. "I've been studying you for a long time."

"You're adorable," she says, smiling.

I don't answer. I just nod and blush a little.

"But there's something missing," she says, after she has gazed at the picnic table, her smile fading away. "There's another thing I love, which apparently you've forgotten."

"I know," I say. "You love books. Novels. But I haven't forgotten anything. Your book is here, in our minds."

"In *our minds?*"

"Yes."

"I've been dealing with books and literature all my life, and do you think this weird thing here will satisfy me?"

"It will."

"I'm difficult to please."

"This is perfect."

"Is it?" she asks, staring at me, expectant.

"Yes, it's the perfect novel. The perfect story. The one we can only write together."

"Is this a romantic story?" she asks.

"Y-e-s." I emphasise each letter carefully, lost in the immense sea of her dark eyes, which are now turning into the colour of either the grass around us or the clear sky above us. It's surprising how easily a young woman's eyes can snatch me from reality and hurl me into a dreamlike dimension, making me unaware of approaching danger or something much worse. Death. Yes, death!

The blade of the razor she's holding in her hand caresses my neck and slashes my veins without me even realising what's happening. I see my blood gushing out, inundating the picnic table, the chocolate cakes, the teapot, the cups, the teaspoons, the stools, the blanket, and her floral blouse.

"Why are you so prosaic?" she hisses. "I hate romantic stories. How can you insult me this way? You should have studied harder, darling."

I try to promise to her that I will, but no words come out, and a bottomless pit swallows me up.

Waiting Room

I hate going to the dentist, and I don't think anyone can disagree with me. Apart from the needle, the anaesthetic, the wads in your mouth, the drill, and that bloody tingling feeling which stays in your cheeks and lips for hours after the main feature is over, there are plenty of other hidden unpleasant bonuses, which mustn't go undetected. For example, you're sitting in a very uncomfortable position at the mercy of someone who is gaping into the depths of your mouth, as if you were a circus lion at the mercy of a lion tamer. Both uncomfortable and humiliating. Besides, dentists wear surgical masks, OK, but the one I went to last year had such bad breath that the mask was useless and I almost threw up on him. Nevertheless, dentists' waiting rooms can sometimes offer some fun if you're lucky enough to bump into a few interesting specimens of humankind sitting there, waiting for their turn along with you.

Yesterday I googled a good dentist in my district. I wanted to change my old one. As I said, I can't stand bad breath. I found one a few streets away. Although I'd never heard of him, I decided to give him a shot. When I rang, a shrill, girlish voice answered me. I asked her for an appointment.

"Would tomorrow at five be all right?" she asked.

"Perfect," I answered, and I gave her my name and phone number.

I was about to thank her and hang up when she asked me, "What do you do, sir?"

"Pardon?"

"Your job, sir. What's your job?"

"I'm a poet and a writer. Why?"

"The dentist is a very scrupulous pro and he likes to prepare what to talk about with his patients."

"Ingenious," I said.

"Yes," the shrill-voiced nurse said. "He doesn't want his patients to get bored. They must never leave his surgery with anything to complain about."

"Remarkable," I exclaimed, and rang off. I was really glad to have found such a sensitive dentist.

As I always like to be well in time for my appointments, at half past four the next day I step into the dentist's waiting room. I glance around and I like the look of the people I see sitting there. *I'm going to spend a pleasant half-hour*, I think. There are ten chairs in this waiting room, but only three are occupied. There is a young, blonde-haired woman, and two elderly people—a woman and a geezer. They are all sitting across from me.

"The dentist is some twenty minutes behind schedule," the blonde tells me, as soon as I sit down. The skinny blue jeans she is wrapped in emphasise her supermodel silhouette. She is chewing something with vehemence.

"Thanks. You're from Eastern Europe, aren't you?" I say, and when I notice a worried frown crease her forehead I add, "I'm a writer and accents interest me a lot."

She relaxes and smiles. "I'm from Hungary."

"You speak English very well, though," I say.

"I've got a degree in astrophysics, but unfortunately I ended up as a call girl."

"Oh, did you?" I say, surprised.

"We were just talking about that before you arrived," the elderly man sitting on her right joins in. He appears neat in his white shirt, red tie, and light-grey suit, almost a dandy. He's sitting with his legs perfectly parallel to each other, with his bowler hat resting in his lap. He resembles what it would look like if a character jumped out of a film produced in early twentieth-century Hollywood.

"And I was observing," he carries on, "it must have been painful and dangerous."

"No," the young blonde says. "Just a bit stressful."

"I can imagine," the old woman says. She's sitting next to the dapper old man, in the same sitting position—legs parallel—but in her lap she's instead keeping her handbag. She reminds me of a female sleuth as depicted in a TV series based on a book by Agatha Christie.

"It happens sometimes," she goes on. "When I worked for MI6, I often slept with packs of men."

"Did you?" I say.

The elderly woman nods. "Sometimes you have to. Especially if you want to dig up super-secret intelligence."

"I meant, did you *really* work for MI6?"

The elderly woman gazes quickly around and nods again.

The dapper old man giggles.

"What's so funny about it?" the elderly woman asks him.

"I suppose you've forgotten most of your tricks," he says.

"Not at all," she replies, and she plunges a hand into her handbag and pulls out an enormous revolver. "This is still my baby," she says.

"You've got style, my lady," the old man acknowledges, confirming this with a slight nod.

The old lady nods a response in kind and slides her piece back into her handbag, just a second before the door admitting to the dentist's surgery opens and a frail-looking blonde emerges. She's wearing a nurse's uniform, but instead of being white or blue, it's vermilion red. Red dress, apron, cap, and stockings. Even red shoes. And on top of that, her lips too. I want to ask her whether she's just painted her lips with blood, such is the vibrancy of the shade.

"Mrs. Eagleston, it's your turn," she tells the old lady, her wan face beaming with a seductive grin.

Mrs. Eagleston gets up, casts a smiling glance around at us, and follows the frail-looking nurse into the surgery. The door closes behind them.

"Bizarre old woman," I comment.

"It seems that we're all bizarre people here in one way or another this afternoon," the dapper old man comments.

"Yeah, right," the Hungarian blonde says, laughing in agreement. "That hag was an ex-MI6 agent still well packed. I'm a prostitute with a degree in astrophysics. And you two guys, who are you?"

"As I said, I'm just a pulp-fiction writer," I tell her. "Sometimes I also write poetry, though."

"Oh, do you write love stories as well?" the blonde asks.

"No. Just horror."

"Oh, I love horror," she says, smiling, and chewing her gum frantically. "Screams. Slit throats. Gore."

"Plenty of gore, I suppose," the dapper old man puts in.

"Yeah," I say. "Quite a lot."

"So, I could be a character in one of your stories," he says, smiling.

"Why?"

The old man bows a little and says, "Let me explain. Twenty years ago, I did in my wife. I slashed her throat with a kitchen knife while she was having her afternoon nap. Then I chopped her up into a hundred pieces, shoved her into a bin bag, and buried her in our backyard. I also poisoned her cat. You know, I hated it. Luckily I was never caught."

"Gorgeous!" the Hungarian blonde exclaims. "You know, I once did something like that. Well, not so theatrical, though. I cut off the dick of one of my clients with a pair of scissors. The bastard had questioned my university degree."

"Shit! And what did he do?" I ask.

"He paid double my fee," she says, giggling. "Or even three times, if I remember well."

"Peculiar," the old man says. "But it happens sometimes."

"What happens?" I ask him.

"You hurt someone and they don't get mad at you. To the contrary, they are grateful to you."

The door admitting to the dentist's surgery opens again and the frail-looking nurse in red steps out.

"Mr. Candybar, it's your turn now," she tells the dapper old man.

Mr. Candybar stands up and, grinning, follows the nurse into the surgery.

"Do you think he was making it up?" I ask the Hungarian blonde when the door slams behind them.

"I'm Cindy," she says.

"OK, Cindy. What do you think?"

"I'm an open-minded woman," she says, "and this is a wonderful world."

"I think he was off his rocker," I say.

She doesn't comment. She just stares at me and says, "Tell me, you don't think I cut off that jerk's dick, do you?"

For the first time, I notice she has blue eyes. Light blue. Almost the colour of a lake's glistening water on a clear summer's day.

"Maybe you really did," I admit at last.

Cindy nods and grins. Then she fumbles in her bag, which is hanging on the back of her chair, and she fishes out a card. "This is my number. Call me if you want to have your dick cut off."

When she sees me hesitate she urges, "Come on, take it!"

"You kidding, are you?"

"Who knows?"

I hesitate a bit longer, letting her wait, arm stretched

out while offering me her card. Then I grab it and shove it into my trouser pocket without looking at it. Cindy seems to have gone off me. She pulls out her phone and begins playing with it. Every now and again I can hear a soft chime or a bell jingling. *One of those childish online games*, I think. Meanwhile, I lean my head back and close my eyes. The silence of the waiting room is only broken by Cindy's phone. I wait, listening to the soft music of my heart throbbing.

The surgery door opens again and the red-clad nurse reappears. I open my eyes.

"Ms. Leadford, your turn now," the nurse tells Cindy.

Cindy stands up, grabs her handbag, and after winking at me she follows the nurse into the surgery room, wiggling her hips. *She's teasing me*, I think. *Christ, she's doing it and I deserve it.*

Now I'm waiting alone. Minutes wear on and I reach for a heap of magazines strewn on an old-fashioned coffee table in the middle of the room. When I rummage through them to find something that I might be interested in perusing, I notice what an odd variety of titles they are. *Crime Chronicles*, *Cold Cases*, *Landru Quarterly*, *Grave Diggers' Tales*, and other such fanciful niche publications. I pick one up and start reading, and while I do this a weird thought occurs to me. Why hasn't it occurred to me before? This surgery must really be a huge one. Plenty of corridors and hidden rooms for sure, like those medieval castles full of secret nooks and passageways. Perhaps it's one of those places where you can play hide-and-seek without getting bored. You hide and no matter how hard they seek, they'll never manage to find you. Yeah, it's damn crazy, I know. But it must certainly be like that. There must be another way out somewhere. I chuck the magazine away and spring to my feet. I must be having visions, though. Yeah, for sure. But what if I'm not? What if there's no other way out? Come on, *they* must certainly have left from some other door inside the surgery. Christ! What happened to them? Mrs. Eagleston walked into the surgery room and never came out, and so did Mr. Candybar. And I bet Cindy Leadford will not walk out of that room either. Christ! In addition, Mrs. Eagleston was packing such an extraordinary piece. I glance at my watch. A quarter past five. Fuck my teeth! I've got to get going now. No sooner is my resolution formed than the surgery door bursts open and the thin nurse in red walks out.

"It's your turn, Mr. Gerrard," she says.

"I've just remembered I've got an urgent meeting at half past five," I say.

"No, Mr. Gerrard," she says. "I'm sorry, you can't leave because in this case you'd have something to complain about, and this isn't in the dentist's policy. The dentist will be greatly disappointed."

"I-I'm sorry. I-I've got to go."

"YOU ARE NOT GOING ANYWHERE!" she yells, like a possessed hag.

I'm frozen in the middle of the room, unable to make a decision.

"Anything wrong, my dear?" a mellow voice in the surgery doorway behind her asks.

When I have the strength to move my eyes from that frail-looking bitch in red to the person who has just turned up, I see a tall, strong-looking man in his mid-forties. His face, his hands, and his white coat are all fouled with blood and shreds of flesh. He is brandishing the revolver that belonged to Mrs. Eagleston, and which he now lifts and levels at me.

A House at the Bottom of a Dark Alley

Everybody talks about that ivy-clad house at the bottom of an alley leading to the dock area, where streetlamps fail to rip through the darkness. Every night over a beer or while playing snooker, those buggers talk. They shouldn't do that, but they can't help it. They know they're stepping into a forbidden land whenever they mention the house. That's why they hope the thick cloud of their cigarette smoke swallows their whispers and their broken sentences.

"She isn't a woman, but a sorceress," a bloated guy says, after downing his pint in one gulp and wiping his mouth dry with his shirt sleeve.

"She never sleeps," another one says. "And she never leaves her bedroom."

"A friend of mine saw her shadow behind the curtains," a third guy says.

"And a friend of mine said he even saw her face," the bloated guy exclaims.

"Did he?" the second guy asks.

"Did he?" the third guy repeats.

The bloated guy slowly nods and balances his empty pint glass down on the corner of the snooker table. "He said her hair is darker than a moonless night," he murmurs. "And so are her eyes. You may die if you stare at her. That's what he said."

I'm sitting in a corner, drinking my bitter. I can't help overhearing their senseless conversation, and I've had enough of it. I knock back my pint, stand up, and walk up to them.

"I can bring you her heart," I say. "Do you wanna bet?"

"What?" the bloated guy croaks. His shirt is soaked in sweat. "No man can do that."

"I'm no man," I say, "but a floating cloud."

The three blokes exchange mocking glances and then they burst out laughing.

"Do you really wanna bet, bullshitter?" the bloated guy asks me.

It's so irritating I don't bother to retort. I move fast, so fast they cannot see me because I'm no longer made of flesh and bones, but I'm only a whirlwind now. In no time they're all lying on the floor, aching, groaning, covered in bruises and bumps.

"Are you still interested in that bet?" I ask.

They shake their heads in unison.

I snigger. "Oh, you've got to be now."

They gape at me, and then they slowly all nod, in unison once again.

"What's your damned name, stranger?" the bloated guy mumbles.

"Perseus," I answer.

It's midnight, the next night. A dreary, moonless night. The whole world sounds hollow as I trot through this maze of dock-area alleys. I can only see a couple of rats scampering in the wan halo of a few solitary streetlamps. I know she's waiting for me in her room in that ivy-clad house at the bottom of one of these alleys. I know exactly which one it is. A biting wind picks up.

"How do you know I'm coming to you?" I ask aloud, and my words fly away in the wind.

There is nobody near me. The voice I have heard has no sound because it's whispering in my mind. I know it's *her*. She's playing with me, but I'm not intimidated and I walk on, and as I do that, the alley gets darker and darker, narrower and narrower. When I can't stand it any longer, I feel I have to stop and my hand touches a door. It's pitch-dark there, but nevertheless I can see the door clearly. It's red and its handle is golden. Everything else all around has vanished, swallowed up by that oppressive darkness, all except for that red door. I turn the handle and the door yields. I walk in and then upstairs. It's dark, but wherever I gaze I can see perfectly. At the top of the stairs a long corridor lies ahead of me, lined up with many doors, but I know which one to open. I push it and this is another unlocked door that yields to my touch.

The room is wrapped in an eerie, emerald-green light. There's a big curtained window opposite the door and someone is standing there. I can only see the back of that person, but it's a woman because a mane of dark hair is covering her shoulders. She's wearing a long white nightdress. She doesn't stir and I wonder whether she has heard me walking into the room. Her hair is darker than a raven's wings. I step forwards and a strong urge to stroke it kindles in me and I stretch out my hand.

"Why are you here?" she whispers, without turning.

I stop and wait.

"Somebody told me you can never sleep because even a breath of wind can wake you up, and I was curious," I answer.

"You're lying," she whispers, and she slowly turns to face me.

Her eyes are as black as two dead stars, no light present in them, doors to another dimension.

"I bet £10,000 I'd steal your heart," I confess.

"You've lost," she says.

I draw closer to her and kiss her on the lips. She accepts it.

"I don't think so," I say. "I know you love me."

"Yes, I do," she whispers. "But you've lost all the same. You've lost your mind."

I look at her and a foolish smile appears on my face. I stagger back, trying to articulate something logical. I long to touch her dark hair, but I can't lift my hand.

"So, my boy, how do you feel this morning?" The voice is close to me. A man's voice.

"*Morning*?" I mutter.

The room is all white now and the warm light of an early autumn sun is filling it.

"Have you dreamt about that mysterious sorceress of yours again?"

I moan and turn my head on the pillow towards that voice. A moustached man in a white coat is smiling at me. An ID card stitched to the chest of his coat reads: 'Dr. Raven, Psychiatrist.'

The Best Poet Ever

It's a sunny late-spring afternoon in Paris, along the Champs-Élysées, but there are fewer people than usual around. This is my first real holiday after a long, stressful year at work, and I deserve it. I'm sitting at a café table outdoors under a tall horse-chestnut tree, enjoying the warm afternoon sun, now and again perusing a book of my poems open on the table next to my usual cup of green tea. Yes, I don't drink anything else, only green tea. I'm a university professor, but also a poet. I've managed to publish two books of poetry, but both of them unfortunately underrated and almost unnoticed.

I realise a tiny, elderly bloke sitting a few tables away has been eyeing me for some time. He's bald, but with a well-trimmed silvery beard, and he is wearing a small pair of glasses. He is also sporting an eccentric, dark-green suit, somewhat old-fashioned, but what surprises me most is the withered red carnation he's flaunting in his buttonhole. On his table I can see a mug, probably coffee or even tea, and also an open book, the pages of which he lazily turns every now and then. Just as I am doing.

Jesus Christ! I think. He reminds me of someone I know all too well. This is out of reality, though. If I were drinking beer instead of green tea, I'd think alcohol was fooling me. I stand up and walk over to him.

"Is it possible you are who I think you are?" I ask him.

"Yes," he says. "I'm the best poet ever."

"That's preposterous," I say. "Because *I* am."

"If I'm not mistaken," the old man says, "your books were poorly reviewed, if they were ever reviewed at all."

"Those were just envious morons."

The silvery-bearded man giggles. "I see."

"Someone I trust," I add, "says my poems are far better than yours."

"Someone you trust and *love*, I suppose?"

"That is irrelevant."

"Is it? And does she love you back?"

This guy is getting on my nerves. "I told you it's *not* relevant."

"It is," he protests. "Listen, it's very easy to grasp. She says *that* because she loves you and wants to please you, and you stupidly believe her because you fancy her."

"I said it's *not* relevant," I repeat.

"It is," he insists.

I drop the subject because I don't want to strangle him. "Incidentally," I say, beginning a new topic, "you ought to be dead by now."

"You ought to be dead too," he rejoins. "If I'm not mistaken, you'd be over two hundred years old now."

"What the hell!" I burst out. My cheeks are flushing. "You ought to be a mummy over four hundred years old now. Everybody round here knows that."

While I'm talking, I catch a glimpse of a young brunette in white making for us, smiling. She's wearing a white cap, a white blouse, a white skirt, white stockings, and white kitten heels. Her legs are pleasant to watch as she minces over to us. I forget the old, silvery-bearded geezer, and focus my attention on this young chick's legs.

"The usual literary discussion, isn't it?" she asks, when she stops next to me. "But I'm afraid you've got to put it off until tomorrow morning. It's dinner time now."

"Oh," the silvery-bearded man sighs, standing up. "Have we got chicken salad tonight?"

"Yes, *Mr. Shakespeare*," the brunette answers, smiling and taking his hand.

"Have we got strawberry cheesecake for dessert too?" I ask her.

"Yes, *Mr. Keats*," she says, grinning at me.

"Let's go, nurse. I'm peckish," I say, reaching for her hand and following her out of the hospital garden.

An Offbeat Collection

It's Halloween night, and I'm standing in the corridor, looking at the front door. We were meant to go to a party in half an hour, but my girlfriend and I had a row about it a few minutes ago. I hate parties, especially fancy-dress parties. They are childish and false.

She persuaded me to dress up as a zombie because she was going to dress up as a zombie bride.

"It would be romantic," she said. And I hate myself for humouring her.

We were ready to go, our costumes and make-up perfectly graphic, the car key already tinkling in my hand, when I couldn't stand it any longer.

"I'm not going," I told her.

She made a scene. The usual, hackneyed girlfriend rhetoric. I can't stand women when they say such things.

"If you really loved me," she shouted, "you'd go to this damned party with me."

"You miss the point," I said.

"Do I? What's this bloody point of yours? You're damn selfish."

"Quite the opposite."

"Really? You mean, you're loving and caring, eh?"

"I'm simply not in the mood. That's it."

"Oh, is *that* it? Then shut the frigging up if a stud makes a pass at me there!"

"I'm easy. You know that."

After spitting the usual "Wanker!" at me, she left, slamming the door behind her. I remained standing in the corridor, where I still am now, looking at the front door.

I don't care if I'm dressed up as a brainless zombie, I think. *At long last I'll go out and have fun my way this time*. And out I dash.

As soon as I step into the first bar I stumble across, I see you. You're perching on a stool at the counter, drinking red wine at eleven at night. We have never met, but it's as if I've always known you. Is one second enough to gain perfect knowledge? I don't want to be blasphemous, but someone on the road to Damascus may confirm it *is* possible, and you are a vision in rags. I'm enthralled by your crossed legs in fishnet stockings and your ankle boots. Your heavy, unearthly make-up, your dishevelled hair, and a purulent scar painted on your cheek are supposed to scare people off, but they don't frighten me. I walk up to you without hesitation.

"No party tonight?"

"My boyfriend went alone. We had a row and we split up."

"My girlfriend went alone as well. We had a row too, and maybe we'll split up."

"I'm sorry," you say.

"I'm sorry for *you*," I replicate.

"Don't be. He was lucky."

"Was he?"

You take a sip of wine and say, "I make away with guys more often than I throw away tissues when I've got a bad cold."

You pause for a few seconds, sipping some more of your wine and studying me. Your eyes are big and lively.

"Is this a sign?" I ask.

You put down your glass and smile. "Yes. I'm a 'zombie' who hates parties. And you're a 'zombie' who hates parties too, I suppose."

"Yeah, parties are false. Just false fun," I say.

"Especially on Halloween night," you point out. "Fake blood. Fake horror. Fake fun. Fake emotions. Everything's fake."

"Yeah," I say. "I'm fed up with fake things."

"I'm fed up with fake things too." Your smile broadens. "I am *real* instead."

"What do you mean?"

"Real blood. Real horror. Real fun. Real emotions. Everything's real in me."

I shake my head. "I'm lost."

You don't add anything. You just open your hand-bag, which was placed on the counter next to your glass of red wine, and pull out a small round object similar to an orange.

"What is it?" I ask.

"It's the mummified head of one of my lovers," you say. "I've got many others at my place. Do you fancy seeing my collection? It's fun."

Rain at Midnight

At bedtime, after drinking his customary hit of whisky, he usually reads "Frost at Midnight" by Samuel Taylor Coleridge. He has always wanted to be a poet and he is addicted to those lines. Especially the opening one, which he thinks has a satanic, aphrodisiac power. *The frost performs its secret ministry.* The frost has to perform its own secret ministry as much as he is forced to perform his. Whenever he reads those words and repeats them aloud over and over again, he thinks of her, lying in bed in her silk nightdress. Yes. Her white nightdress; her white cheeks, breasts, legs; her warm breath. Perhaps the fact she has been avoiding him for such a long time is driving him mad. Perhaps he is either drunk or insane, but he does not care. The more she says she is exhausted because she has worked all day long to make her deadlines, the more he wants her in a way which is reminiscent of a demon wanting his victim rather than a husband desiring his beautiful wife.

How long has this cruel game been going on? He remembers everything started soon after their honeymoon, but he has never understood why. He both loves it and loathes it, though. Especially tonight, because there is something uncanny in the air. What he has to perform tonight is more exciting than usual because it is raining hard outside. It is well known how pleasant it is to be in bed on a pouring night, when the rain is endlessly drumming on the windowpanes. However, he knows it is far more pleasant to watch her sleeping, to listen to the soft melody of her peaceful breathing, and smell the sylvan fragrance of her long, dark hair strewn on her pillow. But the most pleasant thing is to creep up to her, pull her hair aside, and kiss her on the neck. This is the moment he loves the most—when his mouth draws closer and closer to her white neck.

"What are you doing?" she mumbles, opening her eyes slowly. "Why are you waking me up? You know I've got to get up early in the morning. I've got dozens of deadlines to meet at the office tomorrow."

"I would die without you," he says, wiping his mouth with his hand.

"So, it's true you'd never get tired of me?"

"Why should I?" he asks.

"Because you might think my work is more important to me than you are," she sighs, turning her head on the pillow and looking up at him with bleary eyes. "I'm sure I'm not giving you enough. You deserve more."

"Babe, you're giving me the most precious thing you have."

"Am I?"

"How could I live without *biting* you?"

"Oh, again," she sighs, yawning. "I thought I'd taken the usual precautions."

"You mean, all those *white things* you usually lay around your bed on full-moon nights to stop me?" he asks.

"Yes," she murmurs, turning her head away from him. "I'm sorry but I need to sleep. You know that well, but you keep insisting, and I've got to protect myself."

"No, babe," he says. "Tonight you're not protected. Remember?"

"What?"

"You told me you were in a hurry yesterday and you forgot to buy the garlic."

Bad Dreams

He turns his head on the pillow and opens his eyes. He casts a weary glance at the alarm: 3:40. The light in the living room is on. He drags himself out of bed and walks in there. She is sitting on the sofa. She is wearing a sexy sling nightdress, which she has never had on before. For a few moments he admires her chiselled legs, and her toned arms and shoulders. He wonders why she is not in bed with him because right now he feels he wants her, but he is afraid to make his move. He realises he has had this uneasy feeling for some time. She has not allowed him to touch her for months, but he does not even remember why she started rejecting him.

The TV is on, but hardly any sound can be heard, and she is staring at the screen, where indistinct images of war are rolling by. Women and children crying, debris of a house, clouds of dust, spirals of smoke, ambulances speeding away, soldiers patrolling the streets. The breaking-news ticker reads, 'Terror Attack: two bombs went off at midday at Market Square, killed seventeen.' He draws closer to her, yearning to touch her hair, but he refrains at the last moment. She neither budges nor turns her head.

"It's very late," he says, "why are you still watching the TV? Those things disturb you. You'll never be able to change what's going on round the world, but it'll only drive you mad."

"I detest selfish people," she says, without turning her head.

"You've been watching TV all day. Besides, I'm not selfish."

"What's your alternative? Carry on living as if nothing was happening. As if nothing had happened?"

"The fact is," he says, "stress is killing you."

"The fact is," she says, without bothering to look at him, "I'm not watching anything. I've just had an awful dream. I couldn't sleep and I got up. That's it."

"Is it the usual dream?"

She nods. "I dreamt you were no longer here. Again. It's been haunting me."

He draws closer to her and his urge to touch her hair is overwhelming. "Your job is really stressing you out."

"You've got no right to judge me. You've always lived in clover, and you know nothing about me."

"I'm not judging you," he says. "I'm only feeling for you, and I'm suffering because I can't stand seeing you wearing yourself out like this."

She nods again, still without turning her head to look at him. "Yes. I'm under horrific pressure. My job and what I've done. I've been having this same weird dream for over two months now."

"But it's just a dream," he adds.

"You know it is *not*," she says.

"Why are you saying that?" he asks. "I'm still here with you. I'm not going anywhere."

She goes on pretending to watch the TV and she does not turn her head. "Sure you're not."

"So what then?"

"Why can't you get your head around this simple

fact?" she says. Annoyance is flickering in her voice now.

"What fact?" he asks.

She turns her head and faces him this time. He sees an unearthly sneer carved on her wan lips.

"You've been buried in the garden, beneath my favourite rose bush, since I found out you had been cheating on me," she says. "I poured some strychnine into your morning tea, remember?"

Shambles in the Basement

You turn around and face me. We've been arguing for over an hour, and I've failed to convince you. There is a cocky expression on your face. You've always got that smug demeanour when you're certain you're right and my opinion doesn't deserve respect.

"Why should I be worried?" you ask, as I'm starting to lay the table for dinner.

"Why?" I say. "Do you think the extravagant shambles you've got in our basement is something that can be easily overlooked?"

You shrug, while I'm selecting the appropriate spoons to match the exotic soup I've cooked for your birthday. This is the only thing you accept I can do for your birthday. You don't like to celebrate it. You say birthdays depress you because they remind you of the passing of time. Old age. Decay.

"I don't think there's anything I should be worried about in our basement," you say.

"Well," I say, "if the police get interested in it, you won't like it."

"Interested in what?" you ask.

"For Christ's sake!" I burst out, placing the silver spoons down, neatly close to the richly decorated bowls I've chosen for our dinner. "You're a brilliant writer. A clever woman. Is it possible you still miss the point?"

"Come on. How can the police get wind of that?"

"*How?*"

"Yeah. They've got far more serious stuff to rack their brains over."

"This is damn serious because you overdid it this time."

"Did I?"

"Well," I say. "I can understand you loathing the blogger who posted that bad review."

"It was horrible and preposterous. He was utterly unable to grasp the subtle nuances of my latest work. How could he dare say my romantic scenes were lacking in sentimental tension? He even wrote the chemistry was *unsubstantial*. Yes, he used that meaningless adjective."

"Yeah, he went overboard, I know. And I can also understand why that nasty woman who cracked a tactless joke at that public reading last month upset you so much."

"You were there, weren't you? You heard what she said, didn't you? And those people giggling because of her elementary humour. How offensive it was!"

"Yes, yes," I say. "And even that guy who made a flawed assumption online. He deserved it too. I thought he was out of his mind when he dared teach you that sarcastic lesson on foreign politics on his website."

"Please don't bring it up. Please."

"No, no, OK. And then even those other two guys, honey, although I don't remember what the hell they did."

"They all deserved it," you sneer. "Didn't they?"

"Yes, yes, they did, honey," I say. "But was it really necessary to kidnap them, cage them up, and let them starve to death in our basement?"

What Fountain Pens Are Used For

I'm sitting on the sofa, watching TV and waiting for you. A glass of gin in hand. I'm enjoying the evening as I've had a long, hard day, but I've managed to get home before you. You're late, but I'm neither surprised nor worried because you've often been late. You've been working harder than usual recently. I hear the key turning in the lock and the door open. I stand up and meet you. You look worn out. I take your briefcase, hug you, and kiss you on the neck. I only love to kiss you on the neck. No other place but your neck.

"There's the ambassador's birthday reception at the Embassy of Brazil tonight. We've got that extra late-night job to do, remember?"

"I'm exhausted," you say. "I just want to have a warm bath, nibble something, and go to bed."

"Don't worry, baby. I've already phoned and apologised. They're going to find someone else to cover for us."

"Thanks, honey," you say.

"This new undercover job of yours is really becoming a pain in the neck, though."

"Yeah. I thought it was the usual routine stuff. Smoking out a mole at a missile plant."

You look sombre and downcast.

"Everything all right?" I ask.

"By the way," you say, "what did you tell the headquarters?"

"I made something up. I told them you'd been held

up at the office because you had to deal with a serious problem."

"How did you know?"

"About what?"

"About the *serious* problem I had at the office."

"I didn't. I just made it up."

You slip off your coat and chuck it on the sofa.

"I had a violent row with my boss there," you say.

"Do you think he's the mole?"

"Dunno. He just made a pass at me. He tried to feel me up. To touch my breasts."

"Bastard!" I spit. "I'm going to slit his throat."

"There's no need, honey. I already kind of did that. With a fountain pen."

"What? Do they still exist?"

"Yes. He's got a collection of vintage fountain pens in his office. It's his prize collection, which he's so proud of. I smashed the glass case, grabbed one of them, and stuck it into his jugular."

"Perhaps you killed two birds. A bastard and the mole."

You shrug.

"That's my girl," I add. "Resourceful and romantic. I would have used a more prosaic weapon."

You smile.

"That's why you were so unusually late tonight. You had plenty to clean up, didn't you?"

You nod and make for the bathroom.

"Wait," I call.

You turn.

"I missed you today," I tell you.

You nod slightly, smiling. "I'm sorry, I won't be very good company tonight. And please do me one more favour."

"Don't worry, baby," I say. "I'll phone the headquarters myself and tell them about this minor incident. They'll take care of the cover-up for sure."

You nod again. "They owe us. Just in case, remind them we're flying to Washington next week, and that we're the only two agents able to tidy up the mess they've made there."

A Mission to Believe In

Dead of winter. Dead of night. Secret Intelligence Department headquarters. The offices are all empty, except for the commander's. A top-secret meeting for high-ranking officers is under way. A vital issue has still to be sorted out. The whole world is on the brink of annihilation. Tomorrow will be too late. Tonight, or else it will be doomsday.

"The agent we need must be the best of the best," the SID commander says.

"Ten of our bravest men have already failed," his personal aide says.

"It's time to play our winning card."

"You mean …?" Fear deforms the aide's face. "Sir, I wonder whether the cure is more dangerous than the disease."

"We've got no other choice," the SID commander says.

"We might be in for serious trouble," an air-force general says.

"We can't predict what price we'll have to pay," an army general says.

The SID commander bangs his fist on his desk. "*She* is our only way out. Call *her* in!"

Her codename is Gyrdriful.[1] Nobody knows her real name, her age, or where she comes from. When she struts into the SID commander's office an hour later, the eyes of all those high-ranking officers are

1. *Gyrdriful* is derived from *Geirdriful*, who is a Valkyrie in Norse mythology.

locked onto her. She is not the powerful-looking woman everybody expected. She is quite frail-looking and petite, but her gait and her fleece of black hair waving as she walks inspires awe and respect. Her outfit turns her into a Gothic warrior. Black boots, black trousers, a long black leather coat, and shades despite the room being dimly lit. Her black lipstick adds a finishing, nightmarish touch to the whole picture. Although a few of those people gathered in that room may harbour doubts about her abilities, none of them dare to voice these.

She stops in front of the commander's desk without uttering a word. He hands her an envelope. She snatches it, pulls out some documents, glances at them without taking off her sunglasses, slides them back, and chucks the envelope into her coat pocket.

"I want a hundred billion dollars," she says, her voice a hoarse whisper. "And I'm cheap."

"That's crazy!" the army general snarls.

"How dare you? You were kicked out of the SID," the aide tells her.

The commander silences them with a slight wave of his hand, and then starts nervously tapping his fingers on his desk.

Gyrdriful does not budge.

"I can't decide anything," the commander says.

Gyrdriful does not react and remains silent and motionless. Her gaze is on the SID officer.

"Moreover," he adds, "you're not in a position to bargain. You should even do this for free. If you don't accept, we're all doomed to die."

"I don't give a damn," she spits, and turns to leave.

"Wait!" the commander says. "OK. I'll phone the president. He'll agree for sure, but we need time."

"Fifty billion in my bank account in one hour," she says, "and fifty billion as soon as the mission has been accomplished."

The SID commander's forehead is glittering with sweat. "All right," he murmurs, nodding.

A faint smirk flashes across Gyrdriful's face.

"That's utter madness!" the army general roars. "This woman is a renegade, and we pay her fifty billion dollars up front?"

"We have no choice," the commander counters.

"Haven't we?" the general sneers. "And then, aren't Valkyries supposed to be tall and blonde? Look at her!"

Gyrdriful moves in a flash. The general has not yet finished his sentence, and although he is a massive bull of a man, he finds himself hurled against the wall with one revolver stuck in his mouth and another pointed at his privates.

"Unless you want your brain and your bollocks to decorate these walls, bastard, apologise to me," Gyrdriful growls.

Everybody knows she means it. A few seconds wear on. Nobody moves. Gyrdriful slowly pulls the gun's barrel out of the general's mouth so he can speak.

"Sorry," he murmurs.

Gyrdriful smirks and cocks both her revolvers. The general's eyes pop out of their sockets, his lips trembling without giving out any sound and his head shaking uncontrollably.

"You make me sick," Gyrdriful mutters, and with a grimace of disgust she lets go of him and steps back.

"Fifty billion dollars in one hour," she adds, uncocking her revolvers and sliding them both into their holsters on her waist belt. "Only then will I be on the move."

She does not wait for either a word or a sign of consent from anyone in the office, and walks off.

The same night. A few hours later and many miles away. It is freezing cold. The wind is worse than a razor's bite. It has been snowing since early the previous morning, and the night is wrapped up in an unearthly stillness, except for a ghostly shadow gliding through the thick forest surrounding this top-secret stronghold—a stronghold on Mount Everest. Gyrdriful is so skilful that she can escape detection. She is now wearing a high-tech *chameleon* combat uniform and a balaclava of the same material, which make her invisible to either infrared or thermal cameras, let alone those enormous spotlights incessantly searching the darkness for intruders.

She squats behind a tree and awaits, watching the stronghold walls for a vulnerable spot. She knows even the most impenetrable building has weaknesses, although that building is a special one. Her supernatural brain works at an incredible speed and makes its decision fast. She thrusts herself forwards, runs towards the stronghold walls, and climbs them like a spider in a few seconds.

Once on the battlement, she looks around. Nobody.

She dashes towards the first door she sees. In no time she manages to open it and hurries down an endless staircase, which leads into a dimly lit corridor. This corridor is followed by another one, and then another one, and another one, and another one again. It is a devilish maze. Gyrdriful skulks around with confidence because she knows the map of that damned fortress by heart. A wide, brightly lit salon opens up at the bottom of the umpteenth corridor. The room is majestic, with a high ceiling, almost no furniture, and just four chairs, one against each wall. She sees a door on the opposite side. A weird door, about ten foot tall. When she hears some heavy footsteps approaching, she freezes. There is no place to hide. She can only rely on her sophisticated camouflage. The door bursts open. A ten-foot-tall creature trudges in. Gyrdriful cannot believe her eyes. The shape of the creature is one of a man clad in a white navy-officer uniform, but he has vulture wings. She closes her eyes, starts breathing more and more slowly, and awaits.

"You!" the creature booms. "You're an intruder, a woman, and a sinner, and you have to die."

Shit! Gyrdriful thinks. *He can see me.*

"I'm not after you," she says, opening her eyes.

The creature's laughter is a deafening peal of thunder. "How dare you? You insignificant flea!"

"Where's your boss?" she asks in a gravelly voice.

"You have to kill me first," he says, and bursts out laughing again.

"So be it," she murmurs, and springs forwards.

The vulture-winged giant is still laughing when

Gyrdriful reaches him, a katana swirling in her hands. His deafening laughter turns into a horrific howl of pain when the sharp blade severs one of his legs below the knee and a fountain of yellowish liquid gushes out and sprinkles everywhere. The pain is so violent that his wings start flapping uselessly, but he is unable to soar up. Instead, he flops down to the ground in agony. Gyrdriful jumps on him in no time.

"I was *not* after you," she says. "You should have listened to me."

And with inhuman force, she drives her katana up to its hilt into his neck, and then leaps away to watch the giant's death from a safe distance. When the unearthly hulk stops shaking, she steps closer, pulls her katana out, cleans it on the giant's vulture wings, and slides it back into its scabbard she is wearing across her shoulders.

She glances at her watch and shakes her head. She is behind schedule by three minutes. After darting a last glance at the motionless carcass, she sets off down the dark corridor that the vulture-winged giant came from a few minutes before.

Sometime later she is standing in the middle of another huge salon, which looks like a ballroom in a royal palace in Vienna this time. She glances around it and spots a sumptuous staircase across it, which seems to be leading upstairs. She takes off her balaclava and throws it away, then she shakes her head and flips her black hair. She approaches the staircase, and although she cannot see where it is leading because it disappears beyond an arched doorway in Moroccan style, she braces herself and trots up without hesitation. A long time draws on before she spies its top in the distance. Somebody is expecting her there on the landing, guarding a huge white door—a patrol of fully equipped soldiers wearing white masks, and behind them a seven-foot-tall, blond-haired giant in a blue air-force officer uniform. The soldiers aim their rifles at her head as soon as she steps onto the landing. The seven-foot-tall giant in blue uniform does not budge.

"Your skills are useless," one of the masked soldiers roars. "We are invincible."

Gyrdriful closes her eyes and starts breathing in slowly.

"I'm not after you," she says.

"Did you hear what I just said?" the soldier asks.

Gyrdriful opens her eyes and smirks. "I am Satan's daughter," she croaks.

These words set all of them off laughing, but in doing that they lose their focus on her for an instant, and that is enough for Gyrdriful to clutch her katana and spring into action. In a handful of seconds, the floor is strewn with arms, legs, heads, and mutilated bodies.

"Bravo, Gyrdriful," the giant in blue air-force uniform scoffs, clapping his enormous hands.

"How come you know my name?"

"I know everything," he says.

"Do you?" she hisses, and she is about to spring forwards, but the blond-haired giant is even faster with his gun, and a crafty bullet hits Gyrdriful's sword and makes it fly away.

"I can do everything better than you can," he says, with an arrogant sneering note in his gruff voice.

Gyrdriful closes her eyes and her head droops.

"I want to kiss you," she mutters.

"What?"

She flashes her eyes open, raises her head, smiles, and runs towards him. The giant is taken aback, his gun useless in his hand. Gyrdriful jumps to his neck, puts her arms around it, glues her lips on his, and bounces back.

"What is it?" he says, reeling, his eyes popping out of his head.

"You said you knew everything, bastard," she says. "It's a *poisoned* kiss."

"*Poisoned?*"

"Yes. My lips are poisoned."

"But w-why don't you—?"

"*Die?*" Gyrdriful cuts in. "Because I'm bad. Damn bad. No poison can kill me."

The blond-haired gigantic officer gapes at her, his pale skin turning brownish green, and he flops down on the floor at her feet. Dead. Gyrdriful picks up her katana and struts to that huge white door the blond-haired giant was guarding. She knows her target is behind it. She breathes in profoundly and as soon as she stretches out her hand to open it, the door yields in. She does not wonder why this is happening because she does not care. She walks in.

The room inside is enormous and imposing. Gyrdriful peers around, but she cannot see the walls or the ceiling. Actually, there are no walls or ceiling. The floor vanishes into a bank of clammy mist, and on looking up only a darkening, cloudy sky meets the eye. Across the room, perhaps half a mile away, she catches sight of a figure standing. When she gets close enough, she notices it is a man in a dazzling white suit with an elaborately trimmed goatee.

"I wonder why you're still alive," Gyrdriful hisses.

"Many tried to kill me but failed," the man in white says.

"This is an issue that'll be resolved shortly."

"I can read your heart," the man says, smiling. "Come to me. I can forgive you."

"*You* are the one who has to ask for forgiveness. I've never met a worse bastard than you."

The white-clad man bursts into sonorous laughter, and the clouds in the ceiling grow darker and more threatening.

"You're responsible for everything," Gyrdriful goes on, and her katana is alive in her hand.

"You cannot do it. I can feel it," he says.

In a way, this white-clad bastard is right. Gyrdriful tries to spring forwards and chop his damned head off, but something in her mind prevents her from doing it.

"You already love me, don't you?" the man says. "Drop your weapon."

Gyrdriful closes her eyes, her grip on her katana hilt loosens, and the sword slips lifeless to the ground. She opens her eyes and says, "I love nobody."

"You're lying."

"You killed the only person I've loved in my life," she confesses.

"Did I?"

"Yes. Many years ago, in a war you triggered."

Gyrdriful shivers all over and with an effort to overcome his persuasive power, she draws her gun from the holster tied to her thigh and levels it at the man's head.

"*You* are at the bottom of all the crap around us," she says.

The man shakes his head, grinning. "You cannot do what you've been paid to," the man says, stretching out both his arms as if to accept Gyrdriful in his friendly embrace.

"No, my dear," he exclaims. "Do have faith in me!"

Gyrdriful cocks her gun.

"I do have faith," she says.

The white-clad man frowns. For the first time since he stumbled across Gyrdriful, he feels there is something amiss. His self-confident grin fades.

"I believe," Gyrdriful says slowly, "that you DO NOT exist!"

"No!" the man yells. "You cannot kill the *Almigh*—" The bullet does not allow him to complete his sentence and shatters his head into a million gory splinters and bubbles. Two seconds later, his headless body crumbles to the floor into a heap of immaculate dust.

Gyrdriful slings her gun back, picks up her katana from the floor, and sheathes it.

"Yes, I can kill everybody," she says, taking a glance at what remains of the man in dazzling white. "Sorry, *God*, but you're dead now. For good and all."

And she walks off as a gust of wind blows that colourless dust away.

About the Author

Phil Gerraud was born in southern England. He lives on the Continent now, where he works as an English teacher.

Twitter: twitter.com/philgerraud

Facebook: www.facebook.com/PhilGerraudAuthor

Subscribe to Phil Gerraud's Newsletter
on his Facebook page.

Visit www.philgerraud.com

BOG

A Thriller

PHIL GERRAUD

"You should thank me," Rattle said. "I've chosen a comfortable coffin for you. You might have liked something different, but nobody can choose their own coffin. That's the rule."

A city somewhere. Rainy streets.

A disenchanted journalist with no job satisfaction struggles to kick his life back on track after a failed marriage.

When he witnesses a brutal crime, he thinks it is a career opportunity and he dives headlong into a madcap investigation.

He ends up in the middle of a nasty affair where nothing is safe.

Will he ever manage to dig his way out?

**On sale on all Amazon stores
and other online shops.**